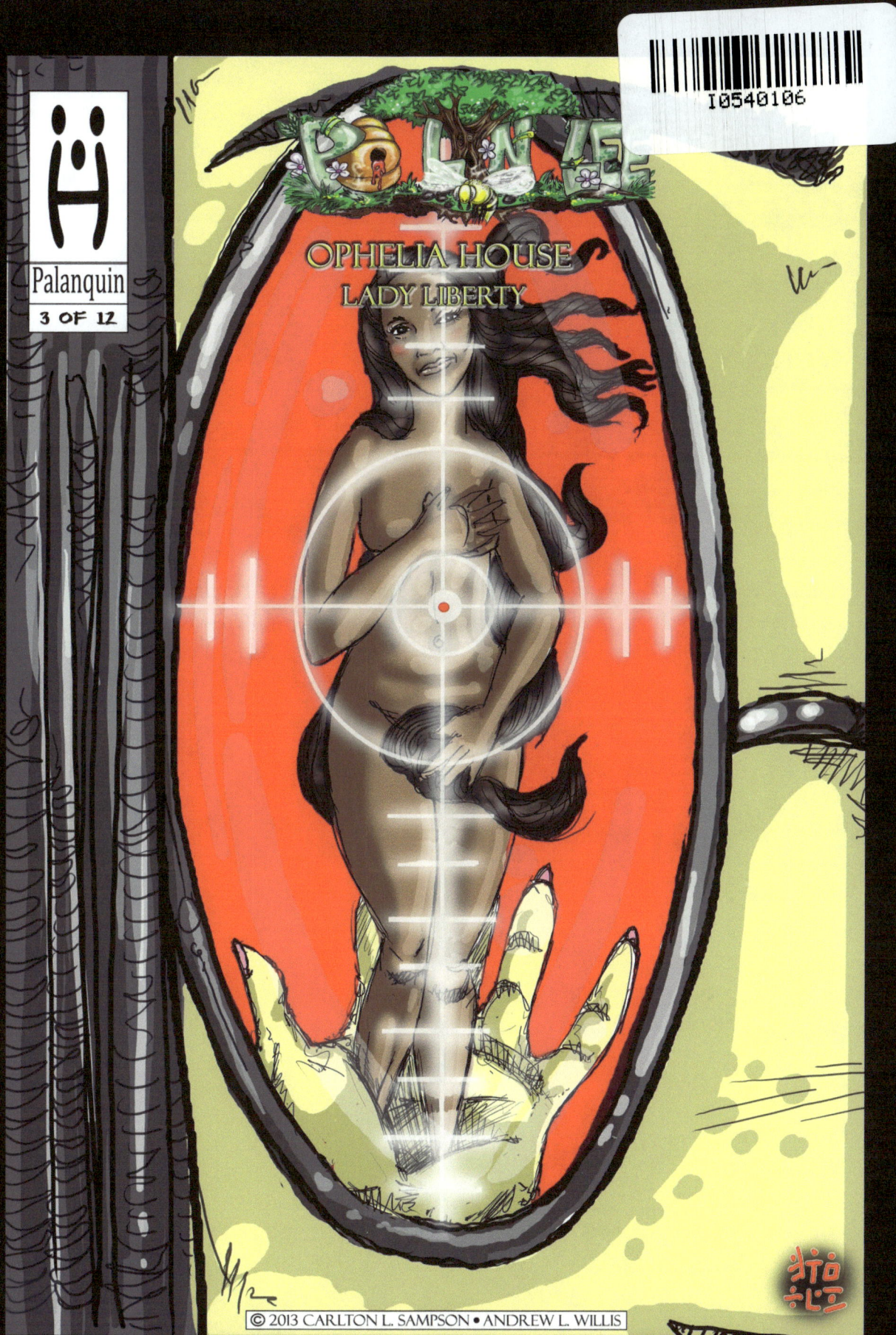

# OPHELIA HOUSE
## LADY LIBERTY

ORIGINAL ARTWORK

## ANDREW L. WILLIS

CREATED AND WRITTEN

## CARLTON L. SAMPSON
COVER DESIGN, BALLOONS, PAGE LAYOUT

Palanquin

# THE WHITE HOUSE

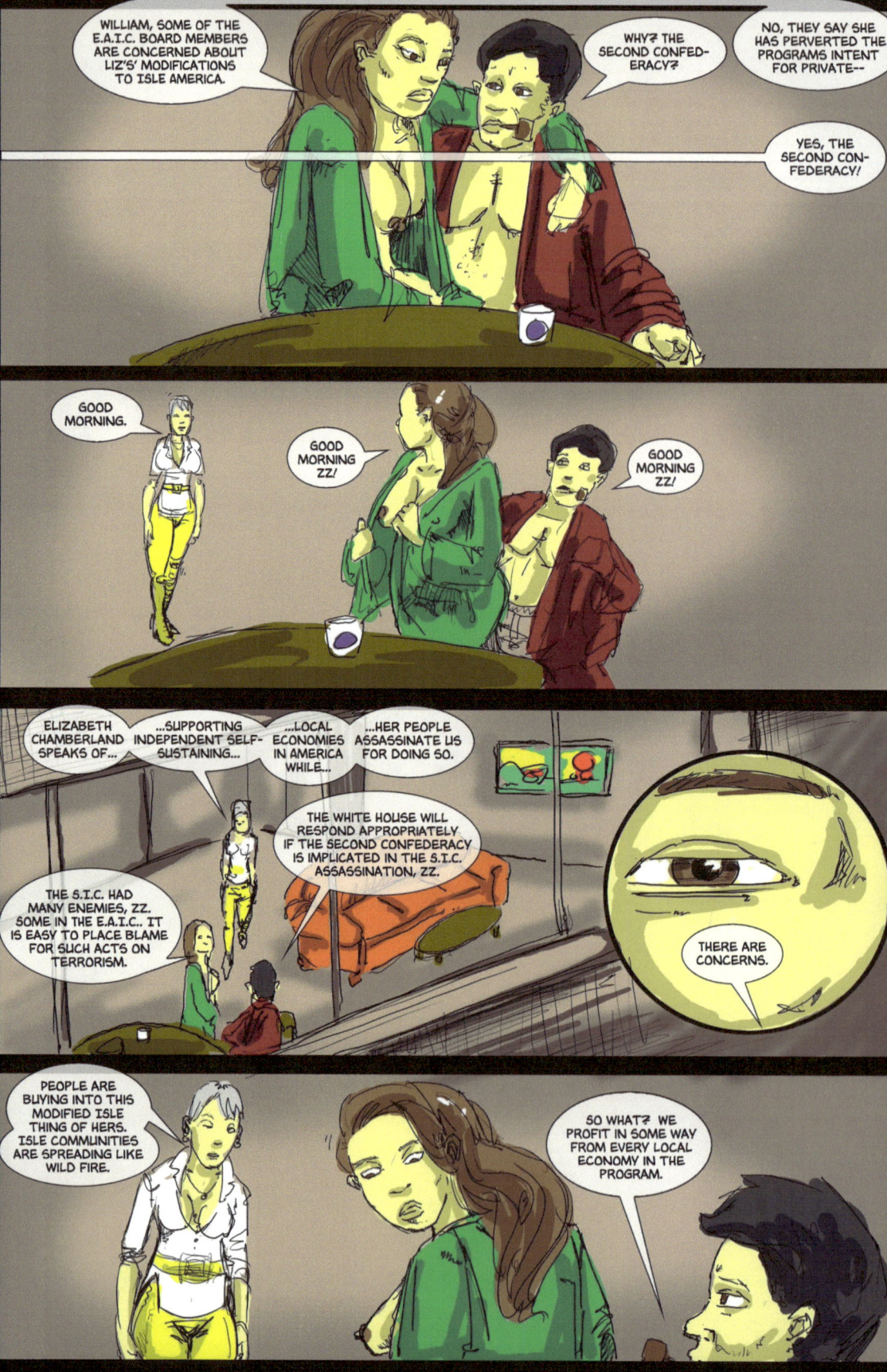

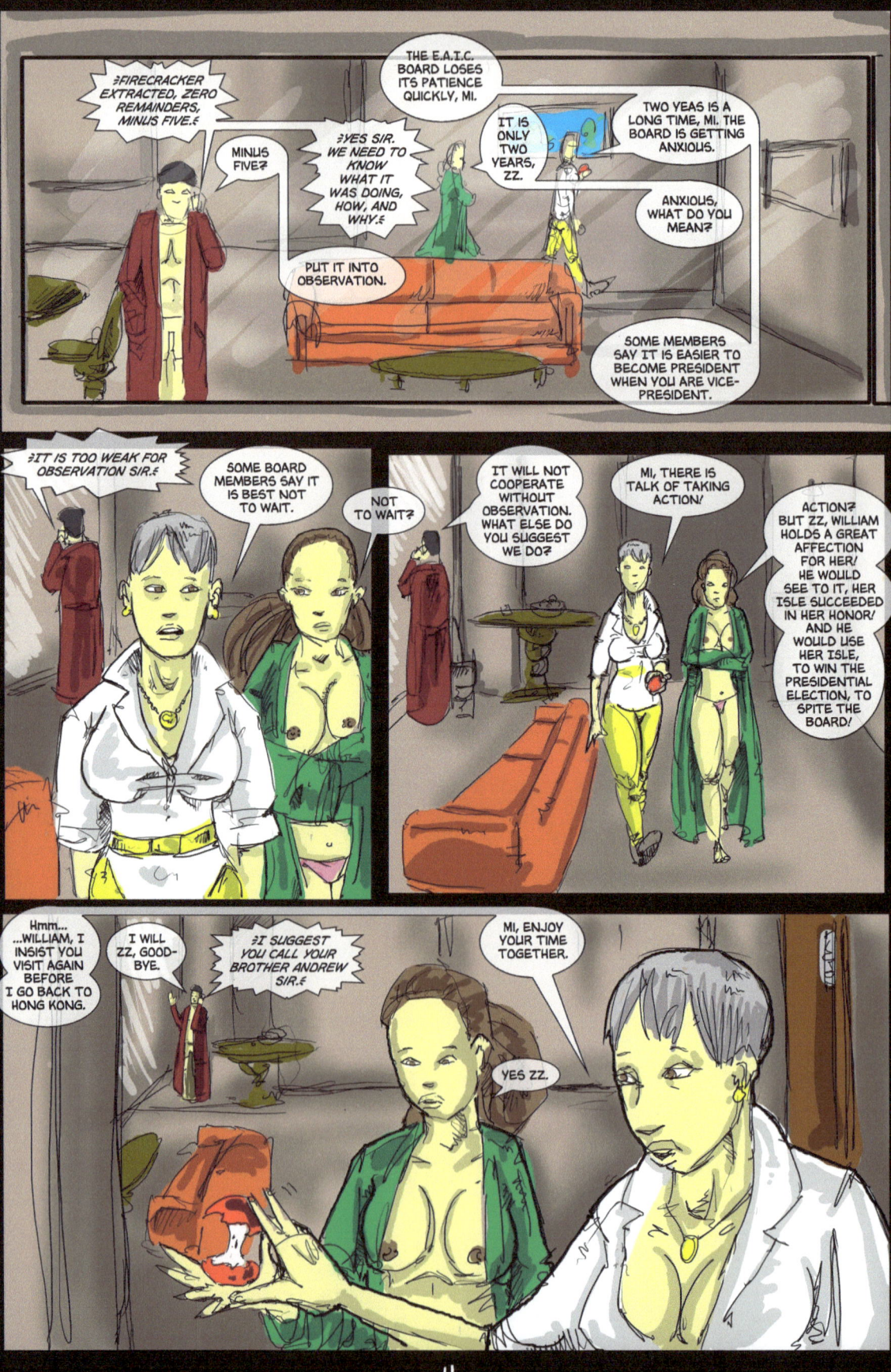

IT WILL TALK IF IT SEES ANDREW, SIR.
I DO NOT GET HER ON THE SECOND CONFEDERACY. SHE HATED THE S.I.C., EXCEPT FOR JO JEN.
Hmm, OKAY CHARLES, I WILL CALL ANDREW. BUT YOU SAID IT WAS TOO WEAK TO ESCAPE FROM THE HOSPITAL. WE ARE MINUS FIVE. I WANT IT IN OBSERVATION.
YES SIR.
GOOD-BYE, AND THANKS AGAIN.
GOOD DAY, SIR.
SOME PEOPLE ARE CRUEL TO THEIR DOGS.
WHAT WAS ZZ SAYING ABOUT MY PRESIDENCY?
SHE SAID YOU SHOULD START PLANNING YOUR CAMPAIGN. WAS THAT CHARLES?
NO, BREWSTER. I HAVE TO CALL ANDREW.
Hmm...I AM GOING TO TAKE A SHOWER.
DO NOT BE LONG.
HEY! WILLIAM! WHAT IS UP?
ANDREW, I NEED YOUR HELP. IT IS MARY-ANNE, SHE ESCAPED FROM THE HOSPITAL.

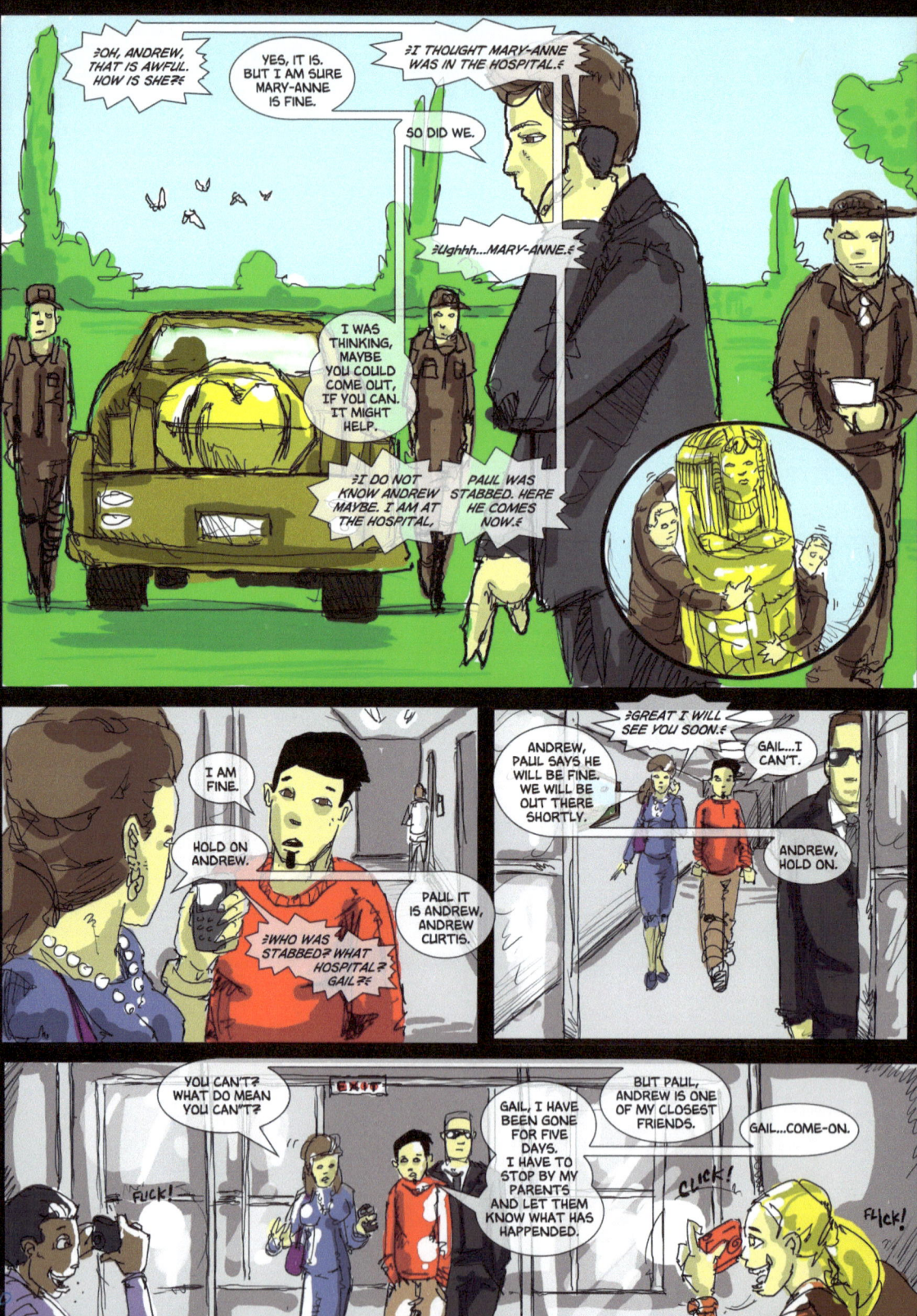

*PO LYN LEE "OPHELIA HOUSE" EPISODE I "THE S. I. C. JOB" PAGE II.

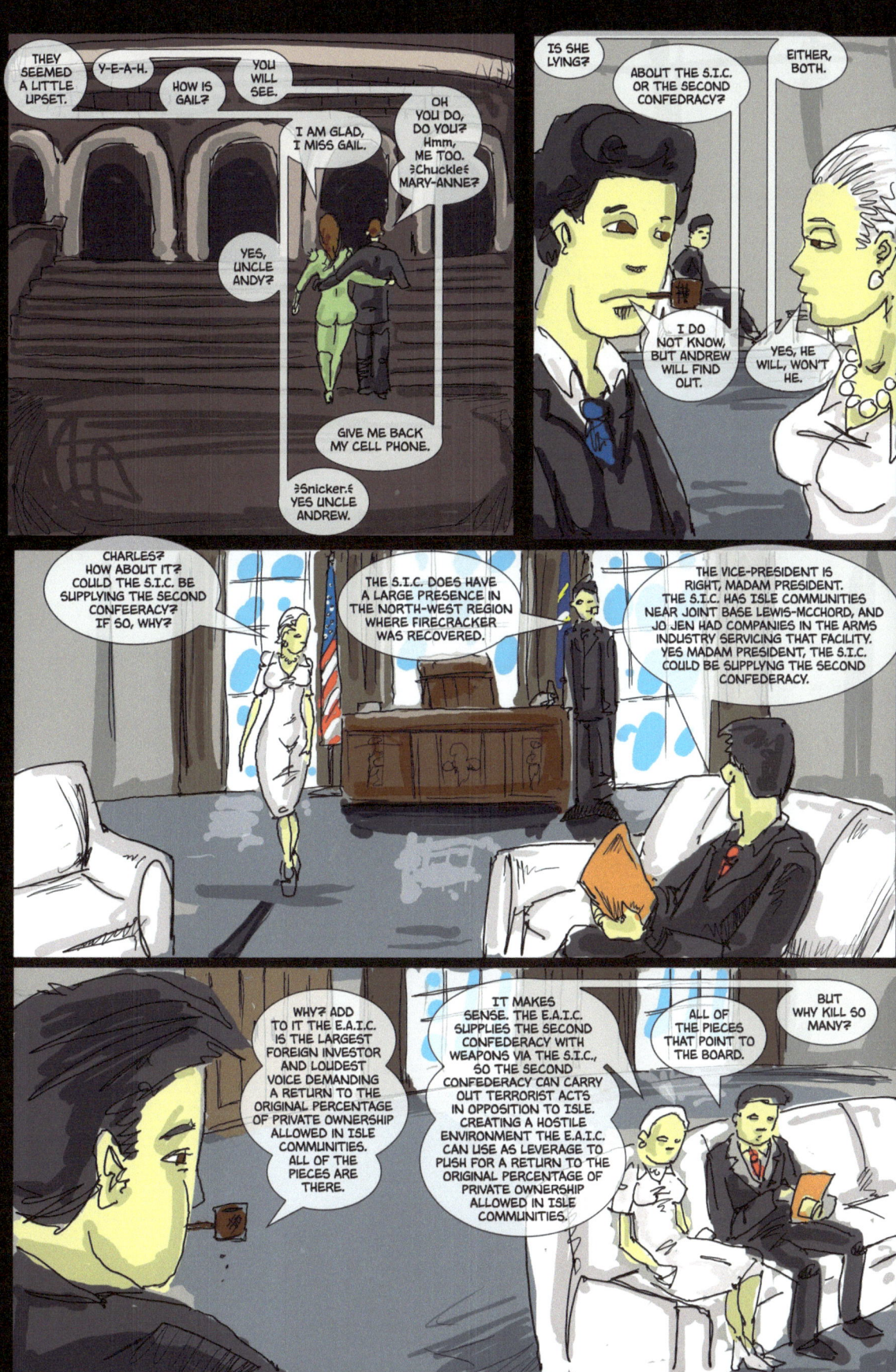

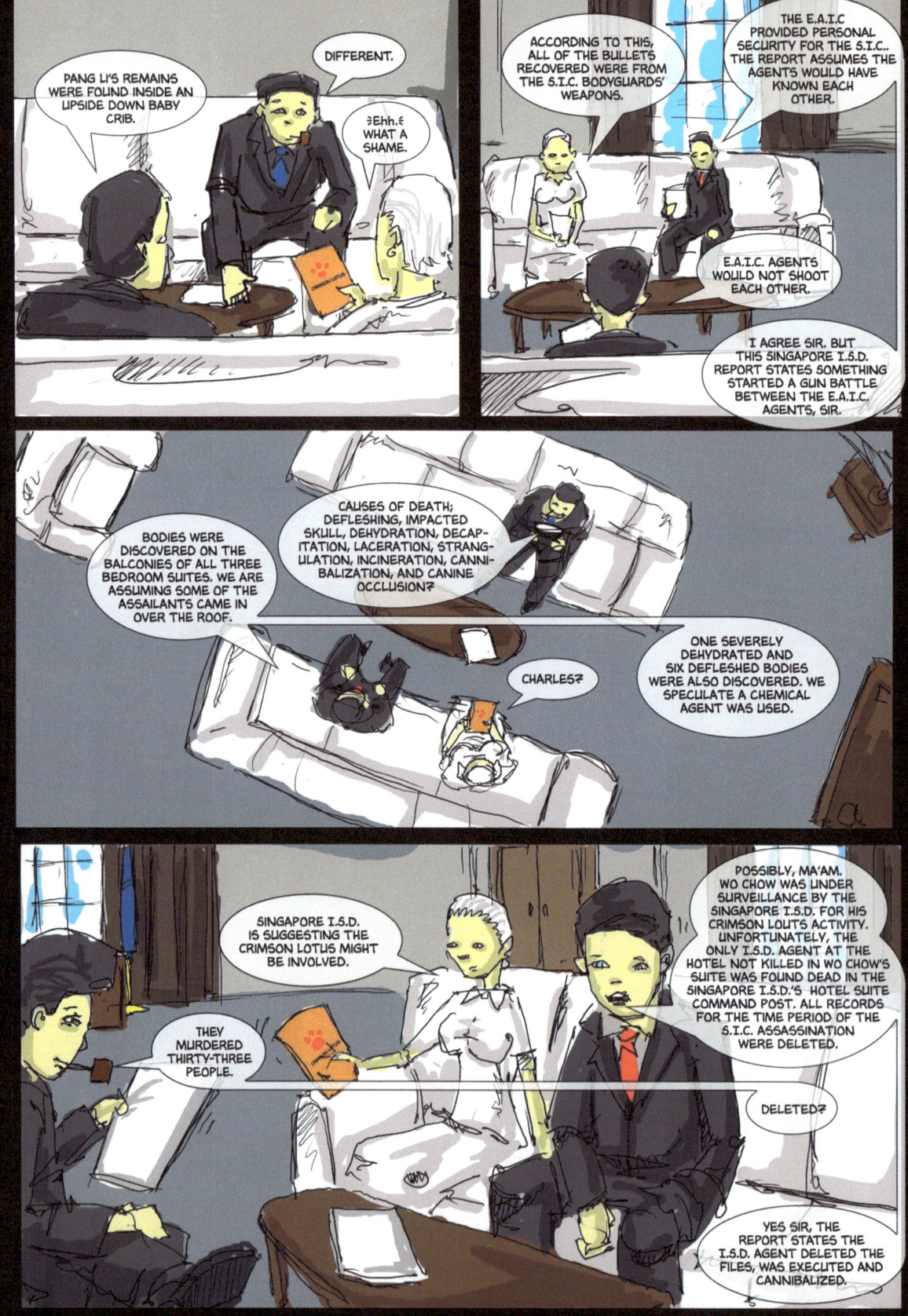

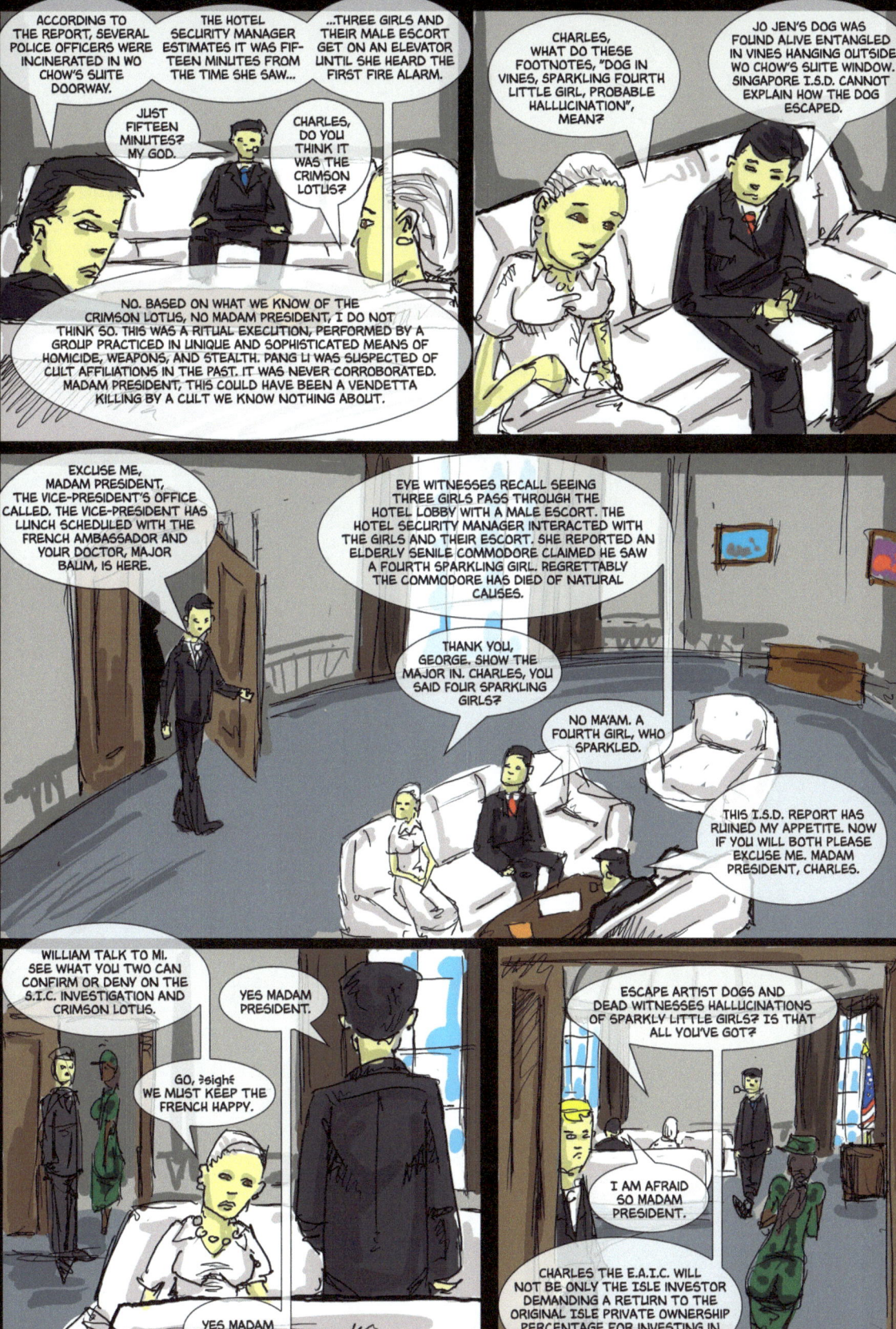

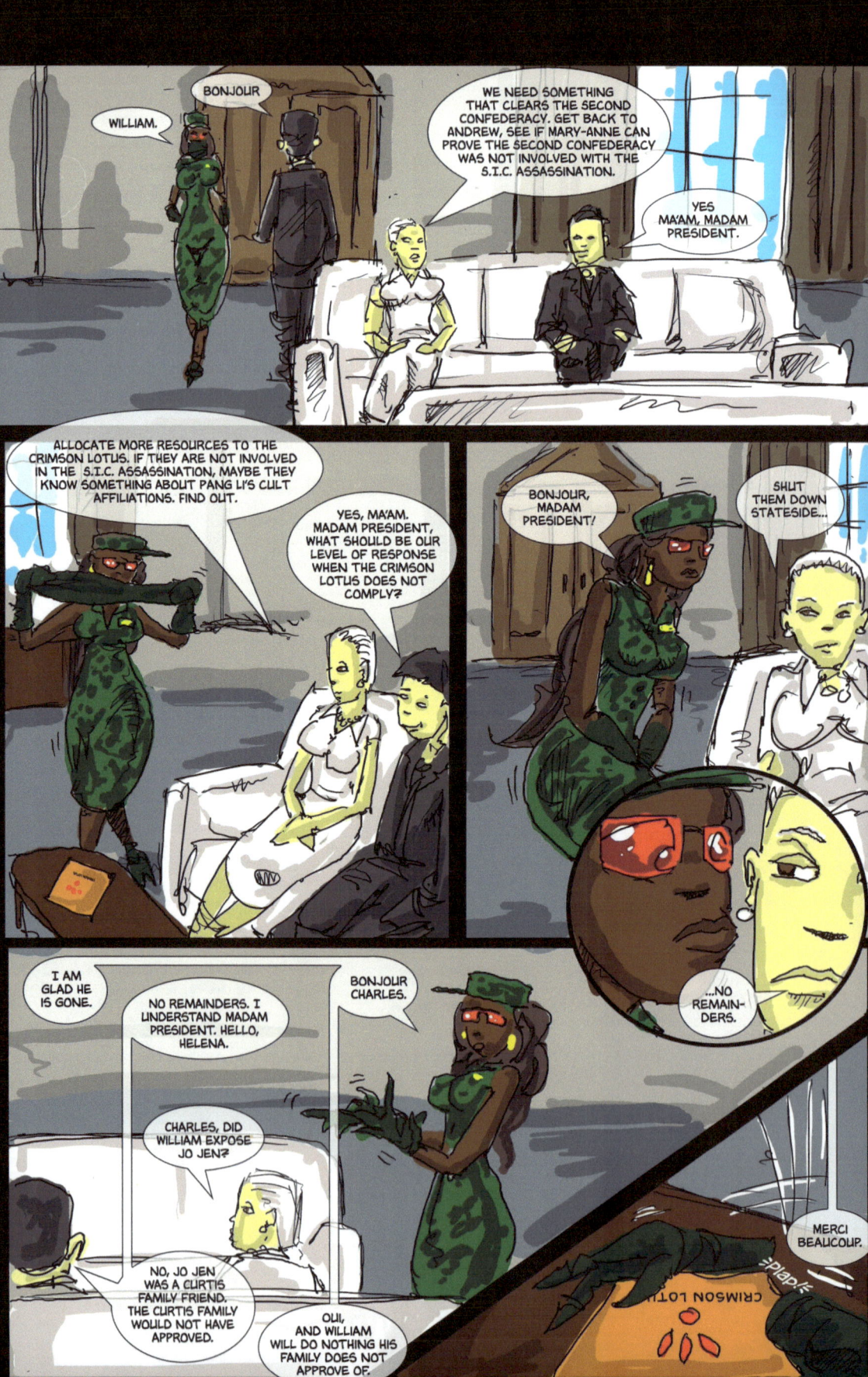

*PO LYN LEE "OPHELIA HOUSE" EPISODE I "THE S. I. C. JOB" PAGE 10.

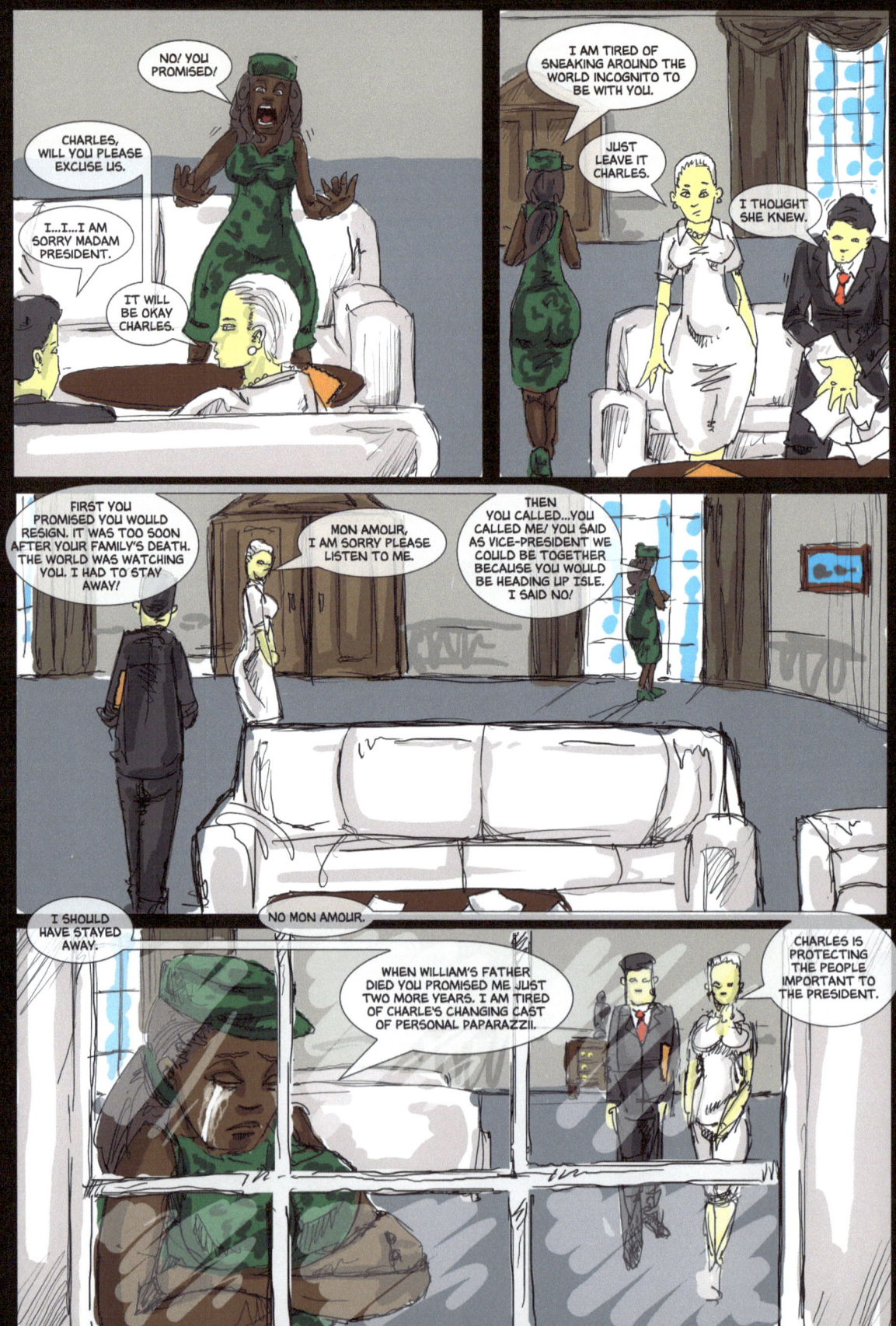

WAIKIKI BEACH HONOLULU, HAWAII
THURSDAY 2:28 PM HAWAIIAN STANDARD TIME.

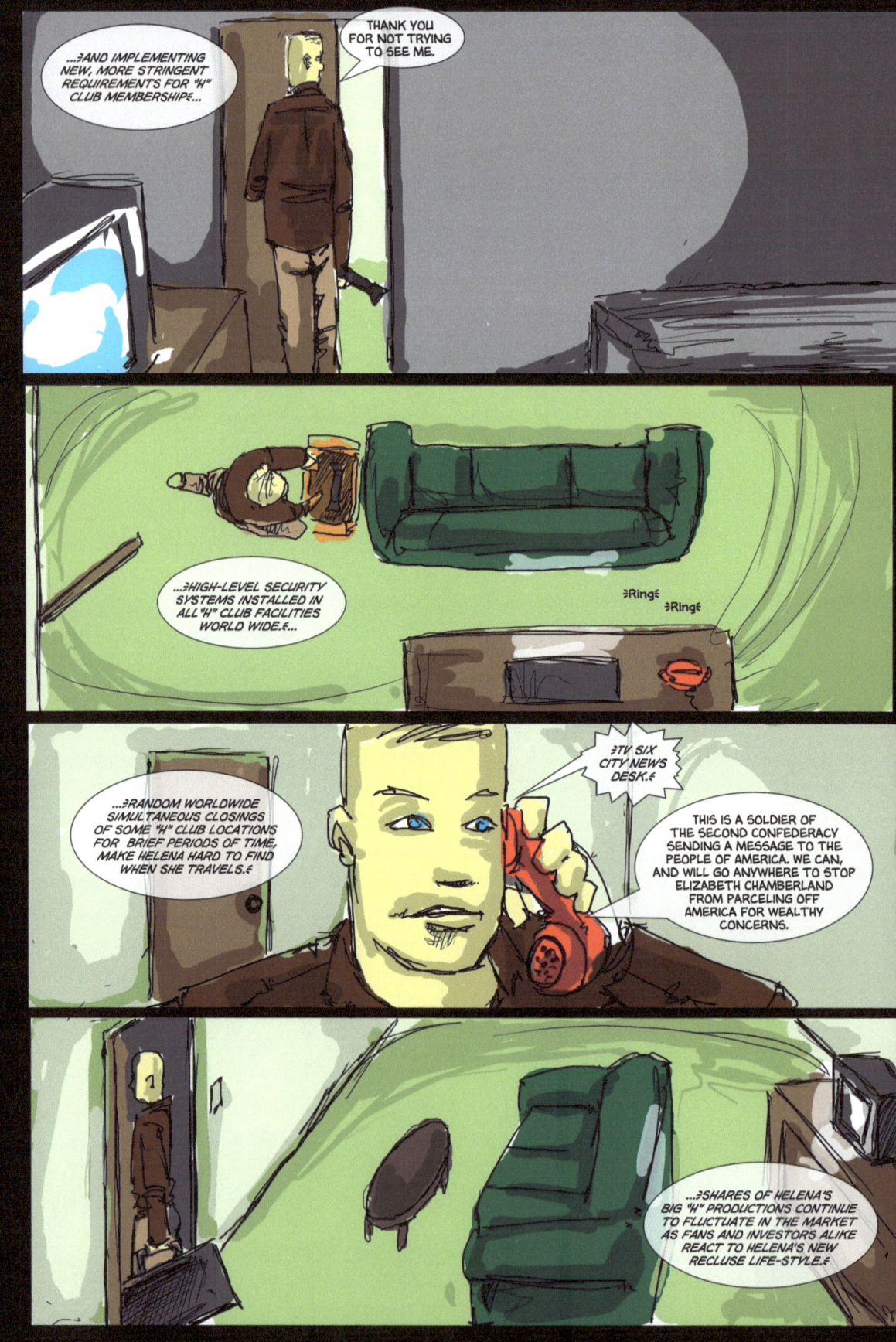

PO LYN LEE
OPHELIA HOUSE
NEXT ISSUE

"FIRST FRIDAY".

PAUL STEWART'S LOCAL ART CRITICS RETURN TO SHOW THEIR TRUE APPRECIATION OF PAUL STEWART'S ART. PO AND MARY-ANNE CURTIS CLASH AT PAUL STEWART'S ART OPENING OVER MEN AND THE MEANING OF ART. THE TA SHEN LING IS SEEN TAKING TEA WITH AN ARTIST FORCING PAUL STEWART TO SEE THINGS EYE TO EYE WITH PO.

CARLTON L. SAMPSON
POET, GRAPHIC NOVELL AUTHOR
CARLTON@POLYNLEE.COM
OTHER WORK AVAILABLE AT:
WWW.PHASCISTCLOWNS.COM

ANDREW L. WILLIS
FINE ART, SCULPTURE, ANIMATION,
MUSIC, AND WRITTEN.
ANDREW@POLYNLEE.COM
OTHER WORK AVAILABLE AT:
WWW.WAOOBAKEARTWORK.COM

PAUL STEWART'S LOCAL ART CRITICS RETURN TO SHOW
THERE TRUE APPRECIATION OF PAUL STEWART'S ART. PO AND
MARY-ANNE CURTIS CLASH AT PAUL STEWART'S ART OPENING
OVER MEN AND THE MEANING OF ART. THE TA SHEN LING IS
SEEN TAKING TEA WITH AN ARTIST FORCING PAUL STEWART
TO SEE THINGS EYE TO EYE WITH PO.

### NEXT ISSUE

www.ingramcontent.com/pod-product-compliance
Lightning Source LLC
Chambersburg PA
CBHW041003170626
46815CB00002B/140